GLORY
to
GLORY

A fictional story based on historical
and scriptural events

D1366574

James Golden

ISBN 978-1-64028-789-1 (Paperback)
ISBN 978-1-64028-790-7 (Digital)

Christian Faith Publishing, Inc.
296 Chestnut Street
Meadville, PA 16335
www.christianfaithpublishing.com

Printed in the United States of America

INTRODUCTION

J UST IMAGINE THIS FOR A moment. What if one of the shepherds at the manger in Bethlehem was a young boy learning to tend sheep? What if he experienced that cold, lonely night so long ago that we have been told was invaded by an angel announcing the most improbable news? What if an immeasurable multitude of an angelic choir joined that angel singing God's praise in the most awesome display of heaven's glory? What if he went along with the other shepherds to find the baby and his family in the stable and witnessed the majesty of God's incarnation? What if he grew up like most shepherds of the day on the underside of life? What if the challenges of life caused him to stray a little? What if he wound up, a few short years later, in a Roman prison facing execution? And what if he met a carpenter facing a similar sentence in that Roman prison? How might his story have turned out? Read Jacob's story and see how he experienced "glory to glory."

ONE

M Y NAME IS JACOB AND I was born in Bethlehem in Judea. It's a sleepy little village where nothing much happens. In fact, big news in Bethlehem is the birth of a lamb, a dog running away from its home, or the local rabbi heard cursing in public. My parents were just simple people who were thrown together by their equally simple and desperate parents. My father's name was Hezekiah and he was of the house of Judah. My mother was also from Judah and her name was Rebekah. We are Jews from one of the original tribes of Israel. Israel was first called Jacob by his parents Isaac and Rebekah but later, Yahweh changed his name to Israel. Yahweh is the name that my people call God. Yahweh made a covenant with Israel that he would make a nation out of Israel's descendants. Our ancestor, Israel, had twelve sons and each had many descendants. My parents descended directly from Israel's son, Judah.

My parents' fathers had worked together as carpenters and thought maybe their first born children could make a life together. So Hezekiah and Rebekah were placed together. Mother brought a dowry of a dove and father brought his baby blanket to the union. That was all they started with to make a life together. They married poor and remained in that condition.

Mother was a capable cook and seamstress and made a few mites here and there making items for neighbors. A mite is the smallest coin that is used in my country. Father worked occasionally in a carpenter's shop like his father but preferred the idle life and the wineskin. When money was short, and it was most of the time, mother and father would fight. And I don't mean little arguments and discussions. When they got into it, there was screaming and the throwing of household items. I'm sure the neighbors heard the noise but nothing was ever said in public. If it wasn't such a disgrace in our land to be divorced, I think they would have divorced before I even turned ten.

My brother was much older than me and was gone out of the house before I had a chance to get to know him. I always figured he just couldn't take it anymore. I never saw him after he ran away from home. Mother told me once after one of their fights that she had also birthed a little girl before me, but she died. I would have had a sister if she had lived. But that was common in my time and very difficult for the women who lost children. I don't think my mother ever got over that loss much less my brother leaving. I think having a daughter around the house would have helped her cope with my father. Her grief didn't help the marriage either. I never really knew how my father felt about losing a daughter or my brother leaving. He held whatever he felt inside himself.

My parents never said much about Yahweh. I know my mother believed in Yahweh, but she never talked much about Him. All my father said was "If there is a God, He never helped me. So I don't know Him." I had a little teaching as a child in school, but my parents couldn't afford to continue to send me so that didn't last very long. But I always knew there was something out there. There was somebody who made those stars. There was a being bigger than us who made the figs grow and the rain fall. Someone, or something, was behind the power of the thunder and the lightning. My mother's father, Father Simeon, used to tell me the stories of our people. He told me how Israel's family traveled to Egypt to find food and then stayed there. He told me how the pharaoh or king of Egypt turned on them and made them slaves. Then Yahweh sent Moses to rescue our people and lead them out of Egypt. He told me how the angel of death "passed over" our people in Egypt but killed the firstborn in every family in Egypt. That forced pharaoh to let our people go. He told me how Yahweh parted the Red Sea so the people could walk through on dry land and escape the Egyptian army that came chasing after them. And then how the waters crashed back down on pharaoh's army and drowned them all. He said Moses led our people through the wilderness for forty years to get to the Promised Land. He said their shoes never even wore out. He told me how Yahweh gave them water from a rock in the desert when Moses struck it with his staff. He told me that the Jews were Yahweh's chosen people. That sounded great but why couldn't He help my folks? If He was really out there and we really were His chosen people, why couldn't He give us a little food? Why couldn't He keep my parents from fighting? I just didn't see much evidence of Him in my life. So I guess I just thought He was way out there and not interested in me. I guess my belief went a little further than my father's thoughts but not to the extent of my grandfather's faith.

I did have a good friend down the road named Daniel. He was about my age, and we played together all the time. Many nights I would sleep over at Daniel's house just to avoid the fighting at home. His parents were so nice and never seemed to mind me being there. Daniel was more like a brother really. We would lie outside under the stars and dream of what we would do in life. We planned to have houses next to each other on a mountainside. We planned to find beautiful wives and each have three children. We planned to be rich and have sheep, cattle, and donkeys on our farms. Daniel was so confident, so sure of himself. He was almost pushy. But I didn't mind. He always had good ideas so I just went along with him.

That's why when Daniel's father suggested that we work with his brother, Daniel's uncle, in the fields to earn a little money taking care of sheep, I said, "Sure." My parents were thrilled that I might make a little money for the family so they readily agreed. They knew Daniel's parents were good people so they agreed to anything they said. I had never worked much because my father hardly worked but I did help my mother deliver the items she made for others. I didn't mind the idea of working. I like sheep and I was going to be with Daniel so it sounded great to me. He was always so much fun even if we got into trouble. Even when we stole a loaf of bread from the woman next door, he would talk his way out of punishment. He had a way of talking to people. I think he could have been a salesman and sold anything to anybody. He was good at everything and I wasn't. He was the leader and I was the follower. So we joined his uncle, Joshua, in the fields.

TWO

THERE WAS MORE TO LEARN about taking care of sheep than I thought possible. I had always thought they were so sweet and cuddly. But when you spend all day and night with those creatures, you realize how dumb they really are. A shepherd has to lead them to the right food or they would eat poison if they found it. And then you have to stop them from eating too much or they will eat themselves to death. You have to lead them to clean water or they will drink swamp water. You have to protect them against wolves and dogs or they would just lay down and let themselves be eaten. They would wander away from the flock and we would have to search for them and bring them back. Once, I saw one sheep jump off a small cliff and two others followed him and all three were hurt. We rescued them but they had to be nursed back to health. But even still, I grew to love them. They needed a leader and I enjoyed being that leader. Daniel liked the animals but didn't like having to stay with them. He wanted to be moving. He wanted to be back in town where the people were. Sometimes we would spend the whole day and night out in the fields and not come home. Daniel got bored and then he would get into trouble with his uncle. Sometimes his uncle would just send Daniel home as punishment, but not me. I liked being out in the fields. I liked sleeping under the stars. And I really liked it when I got paid. I would get a whole denarius every week. A denarius was what a worker got paid for a day's work. But I was only ten so I got paid less. I always took the money to my mother so she could use it. My father would have wasted it on wine. Sometimes she would make me something special to eat as a reward for working so hard.

Finally, Daniel caused so much trouble for his uncle that he sent him home for good. I was afraid I would be sent home too but he said I was a good worker and I could stay. After that, Daniel and I drifted apart mostly because I was in the field and he was in town. We just didn't see much of each other. And when we did, he was grumpy toward me. I think he resented me because he was sent home and I wasn't. Since he was the leader and I was the follower, it kind of affected our relationship.

What was considered the best time by the shepherds was the worst time to me. In my land, the people must make sacrifices to Yahweh to ask forgiveness for their sins. Our holy laws said to kill lambs or sheep or pigeons or whatever they could afford to pay for their sins. The blood of the animals was poured or sprinkled on the altar in the temple to satisfy Yahweh. They said that took away His anger. I never could figure out how He got so mad and then made us take it out on animals. As I grew up, I learned a little more about sin and its consequences. But as a kid, I didn't really understand. Anyway, that meant people would come to buy a sheep or lamb to take to the temple for a sacrifice. It was great because the shepherd would get paid for all his work, but bad because we had to say good-bye to the animals we had come to love. But I figured out a trick. The people were supposed to buy animals without any defects. Not the ones with a twisted leg or a bare spot in his coat. So I would make friends with the ugly sheep with the defects and love them. Then, I knew they wouldn't be taken so I wouldn't lose a friend. They still made good milk to drink and good wool for clothes but they weren't good for sacrifices. They were kind of like a mutt dog who everybody likes but nobody wants. They were kind of like me.

THREE

ONE NIGHT IN THE WINTER, we were out in the fields with the flock. I wasn't quite twelve years old. It was so cold. I had every piece of clothing I owned on me but I was still cold. I usually wore a tunic, sandals, and a turban on my head. But in the winter, I also wore a mantle over my tunic to try and stay warm. I would also wrap up in a blanket my mother made me when it was time to sleep. This particular night, Joshua was keeping watch and I was supposed to be asleep but I couldn't sleep. I don't know. Some other shepherds had joined us for the night and their flock was noisy and I just didn't get sleepy. So I just kept looking at the stars, but I noticed there was this one really huge star that seemed to be moving toward us. It was so much brighter than the other stars that we could see each other even without the campfire. Joshua noticed it too and was watching it as well. It seemed to move and then stopped right over our little town and just stayed there. I know it sounds peculiar but I think the animals even noticed it because they acted differently that night. They almost seemed nervous, if animals can be nervous. Like they knew something was going to happen.

Then all of a sudden there was this … being of light … standing in the sky over our heads. He was taller than the walls of our town and dressed in clothes made of … lightning. I was so scared I just froze where I was and didn't even breathe. He was huge and he obviously could fly. So I had the feeling that he could see any move we made so I just sat there. Around this being of light was this reflection, like gold shining around him. He had a man's head but I couldn't see any arms or legs, just his robe of lightning. He was the most beautiful thing I had ever seen and yet I was scared to death. Joshua froze too and then he looked over at me to see if I was awake and I nodded. I thought we might die and yet I didn't feel like the being meant us any harm at all. It was so strange. He was more powerful looking than any soldier I had ever seen. He was obviously not human. But he had a pleasant look on his face like he meant no harm at all. To be that afraid and yet not worried. It was the most awesome, incredible, amazing thing I had ever seen.

But then he spoke and it sounded like a rushing river after a week of rainfall. And he said the most amazing thing. He said, "Do not be afraid for behold, I bring you good news of a great joy, which shall be for all the people. For today in the city of David, there has been born for you a savior who is Christ the Lord. And this shall be a sign for you. You will find a baby wrapped in cloths, and lying in a manger." That was it. That was all he said but that was not all that happened! Because as he finished speaking, all at once the sky was filled with a billion of the same beings like himself. They all looked like people dressed in the same lightning robes and they were hovering over us in the sky. And then they began to sing and it was the most beautiful music I had ever heard in my life. This was what they sang, "Glory to God in the highest, and on earth peace among men with whom He is pleased."

It was like a choir came down from heaven just to sing for us shepherds, and the sound was perfect. The music was so loud but it didn't hurt my ears. The words were not my language yet I understood everything they sang. The gold reflecting from them was so bright yet it didn't hurt my eyes. There was no way to count how many there were. It was kind of like when I try to count the stars. There were just too many. They sang for a little while and then, just as quickly as they had come, they left. Swoosh, they were gone! And for a moment, none of us moved as we tried to understand if we had really seen what we thought we had seen. But then all at once, we began to tell each other what we had seen as if the other one had slept through the event! Was it an angel? Were they all angels? Good news?

Great joy? I knew the city of David was Bethlehem. My grandfather had told me that when he told me about our ancestor David who was also a shepherd boy. A baby ... born in Bethlehem ... today? A Savior? The Christ? I vaguely remembered the rabbi talking about a Christ, a Messiah, who would come one day and rule over everybody but I wasn't sure. A sign? A baby wrapped in cloths lying in a manger? Where would that be? Everybody had a manger who had animals to feed! Every family who had any animals used a manger made out of stone or wood as a feeding trough. It stayed in the stable or outside where the animals were kept.

As we all realized that the beings weren't coming back and that we had survived our encounter with them, we began to look around at each other. Then we began grabbing each other and smiling and dancing over what we had seen and heard! I have never seen shepherds jump up and down and dance, but we did! Joshua picked me up and kissed me on the forehead and then tossed me back down to the ground! Then when we all were exhausted from dancing and jumping and talking, we just stood still and stared at the sky just trying to understand it all. Finally, one of the other shepherds who had joined us that night said, "Let's go right now to Bethlehem and see this thing that has happened, which the Lord has made known to us!"

And it was right then that I realized that the being was an angel and was from heaven and that Yahweh had sent him to tell us this news! And then Joshua said, "Yes! Let's go! I'm from Bethlehem and we will find the baby if it takes all night!"

So we took off. We had to take the sheep with us or they could have been stolen or killed. So we packed up, herded the animals, and headed back into Bethlehem.

FOUR

WHAT WE DIDN'T KNOW WAS that Bethlehem was overrun with visitors from all over the country. We had been in the fields for several days and had not seen the travelers arrive. We knew the Romans had ordered for everyone to return to their hometown to be registered. Really, they just wanted to know where everyone was so we could all be taxed. But since we had always lived in Bethlehem, we didn't have to go anywhere. But many people did. They traveled from Galilee to Judea, and Judea to Galilee. They came from places I had never even heard of and traveled to places I had never heard of. Some people traveled short distances and some traveled many a days' journey. The bigger problem was there were people everywhere in town. Some travelers had family and friends to stay with but most did not. Most had never been to their hometowns and had no real connection to the place. But Rome required the census so everybody had to register.

As we got close to town, we put the animals in Joshua's pens. He didn't mind the other shepherds using his pen since we were all on the same mission. We had to find this baby! As we got to town, all were discussing where this manger would be. But we didn't know. So we checked every house, every stable, and every pen to see if that was the manger the angel was talking about. As we moved through the town, we saw people sleeping everywhere: in doorsteps, under tents, in alleyways. Everywhere you could sleep, we saw people! We tried not to wake up anyone or step on anybody, but both were difficult with our excitement and the crowded conditions.

Then we stopped in the middle of town and someone said, "What about an inn? Travelers would need an inn. Do you have an inn? Does the inn have a manger?"

He was asking Joshua and me because we lived here and we both replied a loud, "Yes!"

So we headed toward the inn. I knew the man who owned it. He was a nice man. He used to buy some of mother's bread. Since he owned an inn, he needed to have food available for his guests. So he had a standing order of a loaf or two a day from mother. I delivered it to him before I began to work in the fields. I had been to his inn many times and knew that he had a manger. The manger was in a stable that was really a cave around the backside of his inn. The building, that was the inn, sat on top of a hill and the cave was dug out from underneath the lower part of the hill. So I led them right to the cave. But as we approached it, we slowed down. I don't know why. Maybe we were afraid of what we might find. Maybe we were afraid we wouldn't find anything and realize we had dreamed it all. Maybe we were just in awe of the moment and wanted to be careful, I don't know. We knew we couldn't have all had the same dream. We all had seen the angel. Besides, we realized, as we rounded the corner of the building and walked down the hill, that the star we had seen was directly over us. We were so excited in our quest that we hadn't even noticed the star! It would have led us right to the inn!

As we came around the final corner and could see the cave, there was a light just like the angel's light but not as bright coming from the cave. I don't know. It wasn't as bright as the gold reflection from the angel but definitely more light than the stable's one candle could emit. In the cave were two people, a man and a woman. The man was kneeling next to the manger with the woman leaning against him as they peered into the manger. She seemed tired. I realized later she had just given birth a few hours earlier.

Then our eyes moved to the manger to see what the man and woman were looking at, and we finally saw him. The most beautiful baby I had ever seen! He had that same gold refection the angel did but it was much softer, not as brilliant. He was just lying there. One of the shepherds moved a little closer and asked the man and woman the baby's name. The woman said, "Jesus." Then he asked them where they were from. They told us they had traveled from Nazareth and that they were betrothed to be married. His name was Joseph and her name was Mary. They had been traveling for nine days and barely made it to Bethlehem when the baby was born. They told us how they had begged the innkeeper for a place to stay and all he had was this stable. They were glad to have a place to rest and used the manger as Jesus's crib.

The next thing I knew, I was telling the young couple about the angel and his choir … and how they sang … and how they looked … and how afraid we were! They were absolutely amazed at our story and wanted to know more. We told them about being shepherds, about our sheep out in the fields, the star, and everything! And when I had finished talking, I was kind of embarrassed that I had talked so much. But they seemed so curious. Then we all just stood there and stared at the baby in silence. It was a moment I would never forget for the rest of my life. It was like everything was right in the world at that moment.

Was he the messiah? Was he going to defeat the Romans? Was Yahweh really pleased with us? Was peace coming to our land? I didn't know the answers to any of those questions but right then, I didn't care. Angels had told us about a baby, we had found him, and he was beautiful!

As we went back to pick up our sheep from the pen, we woke up every home and every person on the street to tell them about the baby! Some of them were furious with us, some thought we were crazy and some were scared that we meant them harm. But we told them about the baby, we told them about the angel and his choir and the star! We told them everything! And the ones who actually listened to us were amazed! Nobody ever listens to shepherds. Nobody even wants to be around shepherds. But we had the news and we had to tell it. I was praising Yahweh! In fact, we all were praising Yahweh!

I had never done anything like that before in my life. But I knew if He had anything to do with this baby, then maybe I should praise Him. This night had many firsts for me and praising Yahweh was just one of them.

FIVE

A S YOU CAN IMAGINE, THINGS were exciting in Bethlehem for the next couple of months. Not only for the people coming and going for the census, but also for this baby born in a manger. Whenever I was in town visiting my mother or picking up supplies for Joshua, I would go by and visit the baby and his parents. One day, they told me about some other visitors that had come to see their son. Those visitors were from faraway lands and they rode on camels. Nobody could afford camels in Bethlehem. The people called these men magi, which means wise men almost like kings. They brought Jesus expensive gifts of gold and frankincense and myrrh. Jesus's mother told me that the magi told her that they had come to worship the baby. I didn't really understand that but I guess if he's the messiah, then it makes sense. I felt badly that I hadn't given anything to Jesus but his mother said that was all right. But I did visit every chance I could. Then one day, I went by and they weren't in the inn. They had moved into the inn when the crowd settled down and that's when the magi visited. But when I went by, the innkeeper said they had left in the middle of the night. I didn't even get a chance to say good-bye.

A couple of days later, their leaving made great sense. King Herod, a puppet king set up by Rome, did the most horrible thing. Officially, he was the king of the Jews even though Rome still ruled over the whole land. But he had an arrangement with the Romans where he could keep his throne and his position if he did as they told him. He had to keep peace in the land or Rome might take his crown. He oversaw less important matters in the country but lived like a real king. The adults said he was jealous of the baby Jesus and was afraid he was going to take his throne. He didn't want to lose his throne or his power or his lifestyle. He apparently met with the magi when they entered our land and asked them to return and tell him where the baby was when they found him. He said he wanted to worship him too but that was a lie. He wanted to kill Jesus. So when the magi didn't return, King Herod was furious and ordered that all baby boys in the region who were two years old and younger be killed.

Mary and Joseph hadn't been there that long but he wanted to be sure and get this baby in case there was any truth to the rumor going around. The rumor said that Jesus was born king of the Jews. Herod ordered his soldiers to enter every home and search for baby boys and kill them right on the spot. They just ran them through with a sword or suffocated them. If the parents interfered, they would be arrested. It was a despicable act! Mary and Joseph had just escaped with Jesus before the soldiers came. I don't know how they knew to leave but many innocent families lost babies that week. One of our neighbors had a baby killed. I never knew how many babies were killed in total but it must have been twenty or thirty. It was horrible. The whole town mourned for months. Even if you didn't lose a baby, you knew someone who did.

I couldn't understand it. Why would Yahweh let those babies be killed? If this was His plan, why did the plan include killing those babies? Why did those families have to suffer for His plan? Why did a horrible man like Herod have the power to do that? And did Mary and Joseph know that all those babies had been murdered? And where were they? Where did they go? I didn't know any of those answers but I was so upset. My mother cried for days. I was so confused. After being so happy and excited and amazed at the birth of Jesus, now I was just sad.

SIX

AFTER THINGS SETTLED DOWN, IT was back to the fields. But I couldn't sleep much those first nights hoping that the angel would come back. We talked about the angel by the campfire and we talked about Jesus. We wondered where he and his parents were. We wondered if they had gotten home. We wondered if he really was the messiah. We wondered if we would ever see him again. I was eleven years old when I saw him. By the time he could become a king or a general, I would be an old man of thirty-five or forty! And Daniel's uncle and my parents would probably be gone.

It took a while but eventually the excitement died down and we stopped talking about Jesus. We just took care of the sheep. The years went by and I realized that a life as a shepherd was just fine for me. I enjoyed being outside and away from people. I liked taking care of the sheep and knowing that they depended on me. Joshua and I got along just fine, and this lifestyle fit for me. Mother was beginning to show some age but was able to still work a little and keep herself busy. I grew up and Joshua talked about selling me the shepherd business when he was too old to work. I agreed but didn't know when that would be.

One day when I was sitting under an old sycamore tree watching the sheep, I saw a woman walking out of town and she was walking directly toward me. I watched her as she approached me and I realized it was my mother. She had never come out into the fields so I figured something must have happened. As she got close to me, I could see she was wiping her eyes from crying. I got up and walked toward her to meet her. She said she had something to tell me that was going to be hard. I said, "All right." She said that my father had been killed in a fight the night before. At first, I just stood there and stared at her. I couldn't believe it. He was always a strong man even when he was drinking. He had been in fights before but always came home, and mother tended to his wounds. Supposedly, the man who killed him had said my father cheated him. After he killed my father, he left town. I don't know. That's all we ever heard.

It was hard on my mother. Not that she was so in love with the man, but he was her husband for over thirty years. She had put up with the drinking, the laziness, the lack of money. Plus, being a widow in my land was a hard life. There was nobody but family to help out and her parents had died several years ago so there was nobody but me. So I asked Joshua what I needed to do to become a full share employee and get paid like the other men who worked for him. He said I was doing everything his other employees did and so I could get an equal share. He said he just hadn't raised me because I was still young. He, of course, knew about my father and knew I would need more money as mother aged. I began to make a little more money and took whatever I made home to my mother. We made it that way and I did that until I was eighteen years old. I had to work more but I didn't mind. I was grateful to have a job that I liked.

I guess I should have been thinking about getting myself a wife but I couldn't with mother still needing me. She could have lived with me and my wife but I thought that wasn't a very smart way to start a marriage. So I just kept on working. Actually, most shepherds are single men who never get married. They don't usually have any children either. Daniel's uncle was different from most shepherds—he was married and he had children. Every now and then, I asked him if he ever heard from Daniel. He always said no but I knew he missed him just like I did. Daniel could have had his own business. He could have gone to rabbi school. He could have done anything he wanted. He was smart, good looking, and strong. But he had a bad side too. He was mischievous and greedy and jealous of those who had more than he did. So who knows where he wound up? I figured I would never see him again, and so did his uncle.

SEVEN

I CONTINUED TO WORK WITH Joshua and when I turned twenty years old, he made me his partner. Me, a partner of a business at twenty! I was so excited and so proud! My mother was so happy! Her baby had made something of himself! We could afford to have our own cow and a couple of chickens. I know that doesn't sound like much. But for us, we thought we were rich. Cow's milk is so much better tasting than goat's milk to me, and those eggs from our own chickens tasted like heaven.

Daniel's uncle began to slow down. I think he was getting sick but just didn't talk about it. He had weakened to the point where he couldn't walk up the hills anymore like when he was younger. He had to sit down for a rest after he checked on the flock. He seemed to have difficulty breathing more and more. And he coughed a lot. So there were many times when he went home to rest and I took care of the flock. It got to where the other employees came to me with questions and problems. Joshua knew about it and he was fine with that arrangement. He trusted me and I was glad to be able to handle most situations. Since I was now a partner, the success of the business counted on me as well as him. And he had been a good boss and had treated me well. That arrangement went on for a couple of years as he continued to decline in health. I began to wonder how long he could go on. I never asked but I'm sure he knew that I was wondering.

Finally when I reached the age of twenty-five, it was time to talk about taking over the sheep business. Joshua came to me and told me that he was proud of how I had handled the management of the flock and the other employees. He said that he thought of me as a son and that he was glad to turn the business over to me. He suggested that I take over the flock entirely and get all the profits from the sale of the animals for sacrifices and landowners, the wool, and the milk. In exchange, I would pay him or his wife, in case of his death, two denarii a week for ten years. I asked him if I could talk to my mother about it and he agreed. Mother and I talked about it and I accepted the terms. Daniel's uncle had been more of a father to me than my own father and he wouldn't have taken advantage of me or my mother. So we agreed to the arrangement and exchanged sandals to confirm the deal. That is the custom in our land. The parties in a contract or covenant exchange sandals to confirm their commitment to the arrangement. I guess it shows a willingness to be put to some discomfort to make the covenant happen. I never really understood it but that's how it was done in my land.

So I was a business owner at twenty-five! I had made it! I was rich compared to most people! All I needed was a wife and children and I would have a complete life! I was so happy! Mother was happy! We would be all right for the rest of our lives, we thought.

EIGHT

S O NOW THAT I WAS a young business owner, mother began to talk about me getting a wife. It was customary in my land for a man to get established in the business world or community by his thirties. Then when he was ready to take a wife five to ten years younger than himself and make a home together. Now I already told you that shepherds were not looked upon as high class in our society but I was happy to be a shepherd. So I had to find a young girl who would also be comfortable with a shepherd. The search was on! Mother didn't have any brothers or sisters with children so there were no cousins on her side to check on. Father did have a brother in Emmaus but mother didn't know him very well, so he was out. So I began to look around Bethlehem for a possible wife. And that was fine with me. Bethlehem was my home and I was known there.

But I still had a business to run and sheep to care for. When I took over the business, one of the employees left. So that meant I had two employees, and I made one of them an assistant. That way I could leave the flock with him and go into town to buy supplies or sell an animal. But I also could look around in town and see if I spotted a suitable young lady. It was kind of fun. I didn't mind looking at girls. Plus, I had worked so much during my teenage years that I hadn't had any time to look around. So now I would make up for that lost time.

One day as I was delivering a sheep to a man, I saw a young girl working with her mother. I guessed she was about thirteen but wasn't sure. The proper way to investigate a wife is to talk to the girl's father first and see if she is already spoken for or promised to another man.

I found out this girl's name was Rachel. Her father had a shop where he sold household needs. So I went by the shop to talk to him. He greeted me but said she was already promised to his brother's son in Bethany. So Rachel was out. The search continued.

I didn't realize that mother was also looking and talking to her friends at the well. The well was the daily meeting place for gossip exchange in any village. The women would go to the well to gather the day's supply of water for her family. Then while there, she would contribute to or soak up the gossip of the day from the other women. The typical gossip could be whose husband didn't come home the previous night or whose daughter was expecting. The ladies got caught up on the news of the day for the village before they returned to their own home for the day's work.

Mother's friend, Naomi, had a granddaughter named Anna. She had just turned fourteen and was not promised to anyone. Anna—I like that name. So mother and Naomi set a time for me to meet Anna's father. We met, talked, and he said that he had watched me grow up. He said he was fine with me becoming betrothed to his daughter. The betrothal process was a very strict process that lasted from a few months to a year before the actual ceremony. That gave the man time to arrange his affairs to take on a wife and time for the bride to get prepared and arrange for her dowry. So I met Anna and she was nice and pretty and she could sew like mother, so I was happy. I saw her regularly during our betrothal and we talked about what we would like to do together. Then we married in a few months and she moved in with mother and me. My life was complete and things were great for a while.

NINE

ANNA WAS A GOOD WIFE and we had a good life together. I continued to work in the fields and she sewed with mother and they sold their wares. We did well and both businesses grew. We built an extra room onto our house so mother could have her own room and we could have some privacy. It worked well. Anna's parents were nearby and we saw them regularly. They were happy for us as was mother.

Then the trouble began. First, Joshua's condition worsened. He hadn't had much to do with the sheep business but he was still important to me. But one day when I went to see him, he looked worse than usual. I am certainly not a physician but I could tell he was weaker. And then three days later, he died. It felt like it should have felt when my father died even though he was not my father. But he had been a father to me for years. It was really hard to know I would never see him again. That was the first time that I realized that I had grown to love him. I cried for a week over his loss. I visited his wife whenever I could but I still missed him very much.

After some time, I didn't think about him quite as much. I got back to work and focused on that. Men are supposed to be tough and not emotional so I tried to carry on like everything was all right. But the trouble continued. Daniel reappeared after being gone for many years. Maybe he heard about his uncle and thought he could help with the business. Maybe he was just homesick. Maybe he missed me. I wasn't sure. Maybe I was hoping his reason was noble.

But in reality, he needed money and he came home to see from whom he could borrow. He heard about me and my success and came to see me. I was thrilled to see him at first. But then I realized what he wanted. Anna told me to tell him no and to have nothing to do with him.

She had heard of his reputation even as a young girl. I told you Bethlehem was a small town. But he came to talk. He wore me down and I gave in. I gave him some money. I wanted to believe his story even though I knew it was a lie. He was my friend or at least he had been my friend, my best friend. He took the money and left town.

With Daniel's leaving, things settled back down. We got back to our routine and my grief slowly faded. But I couldn't get Daniel out of my mind. I actually felt sorry for him. He had a problem and wouldn't face it. I knew someone needed to talk to him but I had missed my chance. Part of me hoped he would come home again and part of me hoped to never see him again. I was conflicted to say the least.

But then things certainly improved for us when Anna told me she was pregnant! We were going to have a baby! We were thrilled! Her parents and my mother were beside themselves with joy! Now we had to wait nine months to see our baby! Wow, nine months was a long time! Anna did great but I was impatient. I worked but I was constantly thinking of Anna and whether our baby would be all right. Would he or she be born alive? Would he or she be a he or a she? Would he or she be healthy? Would Anna be all right in the delivery? So many questions … so scary. Mother said she would be fine but I still worried.

Finally, the time came for our baby to be born. And I was taken back to my childhood and Mary and how she delivered Jesus in that stable. Now my wife was going to do that. But at least Anna had a midwife and her mother, too. All Mary had was Joseph. And, judging by how I felt at the time, he may not have been much help. Anyway, our baby came and she was beautiful! So beautiful! Sure, I would have loved to have had a boy but she captured my heart immediately. Anna did great and was fine. We named her Esther after Queen Esther from the scripture and she was as beautiful as any queen to me! We were so happy! Anna couldn't work as much but it was all right. I kept the sheep business going and we were fine. It was a good time for us. I began to feel maybe Yahweh didn't hate me.

TEN

THINGS WERE GREAT UNTIL JUST before Esther's first birthday. It was around that time that she got sick. We never knew what it was but she had a fever and a bad cough. We tried all that anyone suggested to try. She just never got any better. Sometimes we thought she might just burn up with the fever. The rabbi prayed, the grandmothers cried, the neighbors brought food but she still died. Esther never made her first birthday and we were heartbroken. I changed my mind about how Yahweh felt about me. I decided He hated me and I felt the same way about Him. It changed things between me and Anna, too. There was a hole in our home and we couldn't fill it with anything else. We grew apart. I kept working but my motivation was crippled. I didn't care anymore. I didn't want to be with the sheep. I didn't want to be in the field. I didn't want to be home.

So I started to drink some like my father just to forget my sorrow and pain. I stayed out late or just didn't come home some nights. I left the sheep with my employees more times than not. I began to understand why my father did some of the things he did. He was hurting so badly, and only drinking soothed the pain. I tried to ease my loss with the same practice. Anna begged me to stop but I couldn't. I guess I kind of blamed her for Esther's death too. I knew she didn't do anything wrong to get Esther sick, but I was heartbroken. I needed someone or something to blame. Yahweh was so far away that hating Him didn't help much. It didn't make me feel any better. But Anna was supposed to take care of our daughter, and still she had gotten sick. Even though it was wrong, I resented Anna. My mother tried to talk to me but I didn't want to hear any of that. I couldn't listen. I was blind and deaf to help at that point.

Then to make matters worse, Daniel returned. He needed money, of course, but this time I was ready for him. I said no three times. So he left me alone for a couple of days and then he came back. Only this time, he came with a scheme and he wanted me to join him. I said no again but I was tempted. He said we would each get half a year's wages with this one job. I didn't really need the money but I was tempted just to get back at somebody. Well ... that is, I didn't think I needed the money.

ELEVEN

ALL THAT CHANGED THE NEXT week. I woke up one morning in my house. I had slept there instead of the fields because I was in town the night before drinking and somehow wandered home and fell into bed. Anyway, when I woke up, I felt funny. I don't mean just hung over from the previous night. I mean something just felt wrong. It didn't take too long for me to figure out why.

I went out to the fields to our usual spot but all I found was an employee fast asleep. I looked around and saw no sheep, no shepherds, no feed, nothing! I hurriedly woke up my sleepy employee, but he knew nothing! He had gone to sleep with a new guy in charge of the sheep. The new guy had only been working with us for two weeks. Normally, I would never have left a new guy alone with the sheep but I wasn't there. It was my fault and now he had robbed me blind. He had taken the sheep, the food, even our staffs. I had a little money in my tunic, but that was it. Anna had still not worked since Esther's death. That was it. I didn't know what I would do.

I went home and Anna and I got into a fight. She blamed me for the theft and she was right. I wasn't mad at her really. I was just mad. I ran out of the house and went to find some wine. I needed to get drunk, to forget my misery and stupidity. Well, who do I run into but Daniel? At first, he avoided me but then he crept over and sat down with me. He could tell I was upset and he asked me what was wrong. I reluctantly told him and he reminded me of his previous offer.

Now I had to consider his idea. I was desperate. I owed for the sheep food I had bought the previous week. And I was drinking away the few denarii I had left. So I asked him to tell me more about his idea. And that request began my downfall. There was this man who was wealthy and had always showed off to the poor people in our town. He had inherited his fortune and had never worked a day in his life. He would talk big when he was in town purchasing goods or hiring workers. I had sold him a couple of sheep once and he had acted so pompous that I almost stopped the deal. Then Daniel heard that he was building a new house outside of town. Daniel also heard that he had bragged about the pit he had dug specially to hide his money. So we robbed the big talker late one night with cloaks over our heads and we split the money. It really was half a year's wages! That was the easiest money I had ever made. Plus, we figured the man deserved it with all his bragging. That kind of money with no hours sitting in the sun watching dumb sheep. No freezing nights waiting for the sun to rise. No nights sleeping on the ground instead of my bed.

Then I stopped and thought about what we had done. I realized I was a thief. Where was my decency? What was I doing? What was I thinking? Then I did it again. And I hated myself all over again. But, as I continued, it got easier. I felt Yahweh had cursed me and this was my way to fight back. I made myself believe that I deserved it.

Of course, I had to leave Anna. I couldn't tell her what I was doing. I was too ashamed. So one morning, I got up early and left ten denarii where she would find them and left with Daniel for the road. That was the last time I saw Bethlehem. I never saw my mother again. I couldn't face her. I just ran away from life, responsibility, and Yahweh. Daniel and I rekindled our friendship as we traveled. It was great to be with him again but my gut didn't feel right. I asked him how he handled the guilt and he just looked at me like I was crazy. He told me I didn't owe anybody anything. He said whatever we could get was ours to keep. I didn't know how my friend had gotten so hardened in life but he had. I wondered if I would get that hardened as well. I certainly was on my way.

TWELVE

WE TRAVELED FROM TOWN TO town looking for opportunities to steal from others. We also kept on the run to stay away from the authorities. Daniel had been doing this for several years and he knew the process. But it was new to me. It took me a while but eventually I picked it up and learned the lifestyle. We went to Jericho, Nazareth, Capernaum, Magdala, Tiberias, and even Caesarea. It was great to see all those towns because I had never been out of Bethlehem. I felt like a world traveler for a while. We kept on the move and robbed when we needed money. But then we always wasted it on drinking, gambling, and women. We had some good times but I still knew deep inside it was wrong. At least I felt that way for a while.

In time, after a number of years, I guess I got desensitized to the whole experience and that ache inside my gut faded. We traveled, we robbed, we spent money, we drank for so many years. I lost track of time. We occasionally got caught but Daniel could usually talk us out of trouble. We never got into serious trouble although we should have. We deserved it but we always got away. We robbed so many innocent people. We ruined many trips for many travelers. We took food out of children's mouths. We stole life savings. We destroyed good peoples' dreams. I wondered many nights as I lay awake when this dream would end. I was aging even though I was still relatively young.

THIRTEEN

ANIEL GOT ANOTHER ONE OF his ideas and it involved me and Jerusalem. It was almost time for Passover, he said. And several hundred thousand pilgrims would descend upon Jerusalem. All Jews were obliged to go to the temple in Jerusalem at Passover and offer a sacrifice for their sins. Of course, my folks never made the journey and neither had I. I had sold many sheep to people as they prepared for the annual pilgrimage. And I realized that I could have made a fortune selling sheep in Jerusalem during Passover, but that was a different life. Anyway, we headed to the holy city.

As we traveled, Daniel told me more about Jerusalem, the area, and the Romans. We had time while we walked to talk. Up to that time, we had not been to Jerusalem together. He had been earlier before I joined him but not me. Since my family could never afford the pilgrimage, I knew Jerusalem only in the explanations of others. He told me that although Jerusalem was the center of the Jewish world, it was under the complete mastery of Rome. Rome had a governor in place called the prefect or procurator of Judea, and his name was Pontius Pilate. He lived in Caesarea on the coast most of the time but ventured to Jerusalem in busy times like the Passover feast. He said Rome ruled with an iron fist and hated the Jews. The family of King Herod was still in power but his son, Antipas, was on the throne now. Daniel said nothing had changed about their arrangement. The center of the city was the Jewish temple, which was a breathtaking structure according to my companion. With its gleaming white stone and ornate gold adornments and fixtures, it was one of the most impressive buildings on earth, he said. He told me about the Jews' governing body called the Sanhedrin, which handled the dealings with Jewish law and the maintenance of the temple. He described how they played power struggle games with Herod and Rome all the time to keep their position strong in the eyes of the Jews. However, we had no idea of the power struggle that was unfolding in the city as we approached it.

When we finally got to the slight rise just east of Jerusalem, we could see the beauty of the city especially the temple laid out before us. I had never seen anything so beautiful. As we paused there, Daniel rubbed his hands together and said, "There's our money. We just have to go and find it." As we began the descent down into the Kidron Valley to enter the city, we noticed a large crowd ahead of us moving toward the city as well. It was a large crowd of several thousand people and many were waving palm branches like they were celebrating a conquering hero or general. But we saw no figure on a white steed, no procession of soldiers, and no fanfare. All we could see was one man's head slightly above the heads of the crowd like maybe he was riding on a donkey in the midst of the crowd. That was all we could see and we didn't think much of it.

As we came through the gate of the city, we decided we would scout around some and gather any information we could. We were looking for accessible homes to rob where the people were concentrated and where the authorities seem to patrol. Daniel said the southwest portion of the city was where the wealthy citizens lived but there were so many people crowded inside the city walls, that we wouldn't have any trouble finding targets. The temple was in the northeast corner of the city and that is where the concentration of Jewish activity would be centered. The Roman presence was quartered adjacent to the temple in the Fortress Antonia off the northern tip of the city. Herod's palace was on the western edge of town. But then all through the city streets and alleyways were shops, carts, stands, and small homes. All of those were perfect targets for a quick snatch by two experienced thieves.

We walked through the city just taking it all in. At the temple, I was amazed to see all the sheep, pigeons, and doves that were being sold for sacrifice. Wow, those prices were sky high! I couldn't believe what those crooks were charging those poor people for an animal that was going to be sacrificed! Then I stopped myself cold in my tracks. How ironic for a thief to be accusing a merchant of robbery. I was ashamed of myself as I thought of my former life and what I had become. Part of me longed with a deep ache to be back in Bethlehem with Anna before Esther was born. With the opportunity of life before me and not behind me like it was now.

FOURTEEN

WE SPENT THE NEXT COUPLE of days snatching items from merchants' tables, grabbing money bags from travelers, and stealing household pieces we could nab from open doors and windows. Daniel had a friend who would buy stolen items from us and then sell them in other towns. He had quite a business going. So we would fill our bags with items and then take them over to this man and sell them. It was easy. It was a sweet deal until we were spotted by a wealthy homeowner. He had seen us around his home earlier in the week but didn't see us take anything. But he knew about the man who bought stolen items. So he got suspicious, told the authorities, and then watched out for us. He spotted us but we didn't see him. He signaled the temple guards and they followed us. As we arrived at Daniel's friend's place, they came right behind us and arrested us. What we didn't know was Daniel's friend had been in on it in exchange for his pardon. If he helped the authorities catch thieves like Daniel and me, then he would be allowed to leave the city without punishment but to never return. He had agreed and set Daniel and me up.

After all those years and all those towns, we were caught. I had never been in any serious trouble so I was scared. The other times we had been accused, we had worked our way out of real trouble. Daniel had been in trouble a few times before we started together but had always been able to get out of it. This was different. The Romans didn't play around. This homeowner had connections and influence. We were taken away to the Roman praetorium. The Romans put us in chains and roughed us up a good bit. They always tried to make examples of any criminals to create a deterrent to crime in the city. They also acted swiftly in their judicial system and many times carried out their sentences within a couple of days. With this kind of crowd, the Romans could make a big display of power and control by punishing criminals. So we sat in their dungeon in the basement of the Fortress Antonia waiting for our appearance before the prefect.

On Wednesday of that week, we were brought up to appear before Pontius Pilate. He seemed like the nervous type trying to act important to maintain his power and position. He asked us if we had stolen the items and of course, we said no. Daniel said we had found the items in the busy crowd and tried to find the owners. Pilate asked us if we knew the wealthy man who had spotted us and we said no. He asked us if we had done business with Daniel's contact before and we said no. I think he knew we were lying but what did he expect us to do? The wealthy homeowner was also there and told the whole story from his perspective and, of course, was more believable than two strangers from out of town. He asked why we were in Jerusalem and, of course, we said the Passover celebration. We had no chance, plus we were guilty. Daniel finally admitted that he had been a thief for many years but that I was brand new to that line of work. He asked the prefect if he would let me go and just keep him. Pilate seemed rather impressed that he actually tried to obtain my release but said no to the request. He mumbled something to his assistant about eventually putting all Jews in jail, especially the chief priests. So there we were—caught, accused, guilty, and convicted. It didn't take long for the prefect to pass judgment and administer punishment. We were guilty of robbery and selling stolen items and we were to be crucified in two days on Friday. He further said he must make us an example to deter others from such activity. We just stood there with the stark reality sinking into our souls. We would be dead in two days. I was forty-four and Daniel was forty-two. I thought of Anna. I thought of my mother. I wondered if she was still alive. I thought of how sad she would be to hear this news. But they were both better off than I was and better off without me. But I realized how much I missed them as my situation settled in on me. I missed my daughter. I missed Daniel's uncle. The more I thought, the more I wept. I was alone and I felt every bit of that loneliness. The thought of crucifixion made me shiver even though I knew I was guilty and deserved my sentence.

FIFTEEN

WE HAD MOST OF TWO days to sit and think of our plight. We had been in such constant motion for so many years that it felt like an eternity just to sit still for a few moments. Plus, Daniel was no joy to be with. He was so mad—mad at himself, mad at me, mad at the homeowner, mad at the guards, and mad at Pilate. He was cursing everyone and everything. I realized that all Daniel had ever known was his own way and he had bucked anyone and anything that had interfered with that way. For the first time in his life, including the time with his parents, he had to answer to someone else in control. This time, he couldn't just walk away and do what he wanted. He couldn't escape this judgment. He couldn't run from this punishment. I realized how hardened he really had become.

When he would finally tire himself out cursing and complaining, he would hush for a while and then I could think. Of course, there was nothing good to think about but I guess I was just trying to come to grips with the inevitable. I was going to die. I was going to be crucified. I had always heard that it was a horrible death. From what I knew, the victim is nailed to a wooden post and cross piece through the hands and feet and then left to die. I imagined those nails going through my hands and feet and felt sick in my gut. I had been told the victim eventually strangles as he cannot continue to push up on the nails to breathe. I was completely disgusted with myself. If I could have taken my own life, I would have. It would have to have been easier than crucifixion.

I thought about praying. But I doubted Yahweh would listen to me now after all I had done. After I had ignored Him all my life, after

I had robbed from others so I didn't have to work, after I had left my wife and my mother stranded without any help, how could Yahweh care anything about me? After all, I hated myself. I certainly didn't deserve any compassion from Him.

Meanwhile, Daniel started cursing again and this time he was cursing Yahweh. I listened for a while but then I couldn't take it any longer. I asked him to stop but he ignored me. Finally, I screamed, "Stop!" and he did. I think I surprised him more than anything else. I had never stood up to Daniel until now. I kind of surprised myself. So we sat in silence for a while.

Finally, Daniel asked me if I was afraid.

I said, "Yes."

After a moment more of silence, I asked him if he was afraid but he never answered. I don't think he could admit any weakness to me. He never had before in all our time together as children or adults. I spent the remainder of our time waiting in silence. But, at least, Daniel didn't curse anymore.

SIXTEEN

FRIDAY MORNING CAME QUITE QUICKLY even though I hadn't slept much Thursday night. If only I had one more day. But I didn't. If only I could see my mother one more time. But I couldn't. If only I could apologize to Anna. But I couldn't. This was the day ... this was my last day. I would be dead by the end of this day. So would Daniel.

Then all of the sudden, the door to our cell burst open and I expected to be escorted out to face my death. However, someone was escorted into our cell and was left with us instead. He was a rather plain looking Jew who also had been roughed up by the Romans. He sat across from and looked right at me or should I say he looked through me. Those eyes ... those eyes were the saddest eyes I had ever seen. He seemed to carry the weight of the world on his shoulders. He didn't say a word. He just stared at me.

Finally, I asked him his name. And when he said, "Jesus," I didn't think anything of it at first. Then I asked him where he was from and he said, "Nazareth." And it was like that word pushed a button in my soul and I was taken back to that stable in Bethlehem in an instant. I was standing there as just a young boy with all those straggly shepherds looking at that beautiful baby. Then I heard one of the shepherds ask the baby's name. And Mary said, "Jesus."

Then he asked them where they were from and they said Nazareth. At that thought, I came crashing back to that cruel jail cell and those sad eyes. Could it be him? Could this man be the baby I saw in Bethlehem so many years ago? Was he to share my cell like I had shared his stable? I had to know. I had to ask.

"Sir," I started, "were you born in Bethlehem?"

He nodded.

"Was your mother named Mary?"

Again, he nodded.

"Did your family leave Bethlehem suddenly in the night after your birth?"

A final nod told me this man was the "baby born to you a Savior, who is Christ the Lord." I couldn't believe it! This man was the Jesus born in my hometown! This was the baby the angels sang about! I told him I had been at the stable in Bethlehem where he was born! I told him about the angels! I told him about the gold reflection from his head! I told him how we told everyone we met about the baby after we left the stable! Those words brought a slight smile to his face.

After a moment, I had to ask him, "Are you the Messiah?"

And before he could answer, the cell door burst open, Jesus was grabbed up, taken out, and the door was slammed shut.

SEVENTEEN

THEY NEVER BROUGHT HIM BACK. They came and got us and took us outside, to the praetorium courtyard. They were forming the detail to take us out to the site of the crucifixions. It was then that I saw Jesus again. I don't know what they had done to him since he left our cell, but he looked horrible. They had beaten him to a bloody mess. He could hardly stand much less carry the crossbeam they made all three of us carry. It was a large plank of heavy wood and we had to carry it on our shoulders. There were many Roman soldiers in the detail. Some of them were clearing a path through the boisterous crowd and some were keeping us moving. The crowd was enormous as we made our way through the streets of the city. The crowd jeered at us and threw things at us. As we got to the city gate, Jesus fell for the third time and the crossbeam fell right on his head. He couldn't even lift the wood off of his head. The Romans hit him with their whips but it was no use. He couldn't do anymore. The whole parade came to a grinding halt as the Romans decided what to do.

They reached into the crowd and grabbed some poor man and made him carry Jesus's crossbeam. He complied and that allowed Jesus to walk on his own but he still stumbled along with great difficulty. Daniel and I had not been beaten so we were able to carry our crossbeams. However, they hit us anyway just to make their point to the crowd.

Finally, we got to the place and it was like a rocky side of a hill. They took the crossbeams from each of us, which relieved the stranger of his involvement. He quickly blended back into the crowd of onlookers. I noticed that there were long shafts of wood each lying next to a hole in the ground. I assumed those shafts would be placed in the holes and raised up to complete the crucifixion process. But how would they attach us to the shaft? My question wouldn't linger long. They quickly threw Daniel to the ground at the top of one of the shafts. They placed his crossbeam under his head and shoulders then stretched his arms out to the ends of the crossbeam. Then they actually nailed his wrists to the ends with thick spikes and, of course, Daniel let out a piercing, cursing scream. Next, without delay, they nailed his feet to the bottom of the shaft where a preset step had been placed and, again, he screamed. Seeing that scene made me vomit at the feet of one of the soldiers. He cursed at me and punched me so hard that I fell down. The idea of a spike going through my foot just turned my stomach. Then the crossbeam was fit on top of the shaft like a tongue and groove and the shaft was lined up with the hole that was pre-dug. They dropped the shaft into the hole. There was a deep thud and Daniel screamed again. I stood there in disbelief as I realized that my friend really had been crucified.

But I didn't ponder long as I was next and they repeated the grotesque process on me. The pain of the spikes completely took my breath and then I let out a guttural scream just like Daniel. It was the worst pain I had ever felt but it didn't subside. The searing jolt screeched up my arms and legs and exploded in my head! My feet throbbed incessantly! The pressure on my joints as I began to hang was tremendous and I wondered if my arms might tear away from my torso. I expected my skin at my armpits to split from the stretching. I immediately understood how a person would eventually strangle from the difficulty of breathing in that position. Finally, they repeated the process for Jesus but he didn't make a sound. As they hoisted him up, I noticed for the first time that he had a cap or ring of thorns on his head. The thorns were pressed into his scalp and he was bleeding from that too. From the crown of thorns, the beating, the earlier roughing up, and now the nails, this man had suffered so much. And yet, he didn't make a sound. He didn't scream or curse or anything. He just took it. They dropped his shaft into the hole and Jesus let out a low moan. Then they hammered stakes into the ground around each of our shafts to secure them in place. At that point, the crucifixion sentence was complete with Jesus in the middle and me and Daniel on each side.

It was a few minutes before I could figure out how to breathe with the least amount of additional pain. As soon as Jesus figured that out, he said the most astounding thing. He said, "Father, forgive them for they know not what they do." Who was he talking to and why did he say that? Was he talking to Yahweh? Was he talking about the Romans, the crowd, or me? I didn't know but I was still amazed. Was that love or stupidity or was he out of his mind? They had already tried to give him a drugged drink but he had refused it. He was completely sane as far as I knew. Of course, Daniel began to curse him as well as everybody else within hearing distance.

I could just see out of the corner of my eye that some Roman soldiers were gambling for some clothes. I guess they were Jesus's because Daniel and I had nothing with us when we were caught but the tunics on our back and they had taken those from us.

There was a crowd that had gathered to watch this gruesome scene and many of them called out and sneered at Jesus. And I noticed that most of the ones who jeered at him were chief priests— the rabbis in the temple, the holy men of Yahweh. What were they upset about? What could he have done to rile them? I didn't know but they seemed to enjoy his punishment. Some of the soldiers jeered at him as well, saying, "If you are the king of the Jews, save yourself!"

They bowed in front of him and mocked him. Then someone from the crowd yelled out, "He saved others, let him save himself if he is the Christ of God!"

It was then that I realized that the circle of thorns was supposed to be a crown. Of course, they bowed to him in mockery only. That was the ultimate in shame and humiliation for this man. This was the cruelest scene I had ever witnessed in my life. Not for me and Daniel but for this seemingly innocent man. There were also some women standing nearby who were crying. They obviously were friends of Jesus. Then one older woman and a young man came up close to Jesus and stood at his feet. She was weeping but not making a scene. The soldiers tensed but did not interfere.

Then Jesus spoke to them. If I heard correctly, he said, "Woman, behold your son."

Could that have been Mary? It had been thirty something years since I had seen her but he said "your son!" I didn't know but then he spoke again. This time I thought he said, "Son, behold your mother." Was he talking to the young man? Was this man his brother? Again, I didn't know. It was so hard to even breathe, much less talk. I don't know how he said anything. After that exchange, the couple moved back down the hill.

The pain of the nails and the stretching of my arms out of joint intensified as the moments seemed like hours. I didn't know how long we had been on the cross, but it seemed like forever. Daniel had stopped his cursing for the moment and just moaned to himself. I had to push down on the small step where my feet were nailed every time to take a breath. It was a shallow breath each time and I knew I couldn't do that for very long.

EIGHTEEN

AFTER WE HAD HUNG THERE for what felt like a lifetime, the wind began to pick up and all at once the sky darkened like just before a rainstorm. Some of the people headed back to town. The soldiers wrapped their togas more tightly around themselves and grumbled about "those stupid Jews." Then Jesus raised himself up and cried out, "My God, my God, why hast Thou forsaken me?"

He was calling out to Yahweh in desperation. I wanted to do the same but I knew I had forsaken Yahweh long ago and He wasn't going to listen to me, much less respond. Of course, there was no real response to Jesus except a big clap of thunder. Then the chief priests began to jeer at him again.

They said, "Let's see if God comes and rescues him now!"

Their hate for this man was unbelievable. I had seen hate before but this collected display was vicious. They were actually enjoying Jesus's agony.

Next, Jesus cried out, "I thirst!"

And one of the soldiers, after receiving permission from the centurion in charge, took a sponge and doused it in wine and held it up to Jesus's lips on a stick. Jesus took some of the wine. I would have loved to have had that moisture on my lips as I was parched inside and out. But Jesus must have been even drier as he had suffered much more than Daniel and me. The wind continued to howl and more people left the scene. I could tell Jesus wasn't going to last much longer. I wanted to talk to him but I couldn't breathe very well. My left leg was cramping and it made it harder to raise up, to take a breath.

But I had to say something to him. What could I say? Could I ask him again if he was the Messiah? Could I ask him if Yahweh would forgive me? Could I ask him if he was God?

But before I could even speak, Daniel started cursing at him again. He yelled, "Are you not the Christ? Save yourself and us!"

I couldn't believe he said that, so I fired back at him. I said, "Do you not even fear God, since you are under the same sentence of condemnation? We are receiving what we deserve for our deeds, but this man has done nothing wrong."

Daniel didn't say any more. He just cursed to himself under his breath. I was ashamed of Daniel and myself. But I still wanted to speak to Jesus. Then I noticed the sign above his head that the Romans had written. It read "King of the Jews." I didn't understand what that meant but I thought maybe he really was a king. From all I had heard about Herod all my life, I knew he was a fake. His father had murdered all those babies. This Herod just continued that same kind of power-hungry, brutal reign. He was no king. And I knew Caesar in Rome was just a ruthless dictator. His representatives here were just as bad. I thought maybe this Jesus was different. So with that in mind, I just blurted out, "Jesus, remember me when you come in your kingdom!" I didn't know what I was thinking. It was like something took over and spoke for me. But then amazingly, he answered me.

He said, "Truly I say to you, today you shall be with me in paradise."

And with those words, I just started crying. I felt a peace inside like never before. I felt like maybe Yahweh didn't hate me after all. I looked back at Jesus and our eyes met and he nodded at me. I was still in unbelievable pain and I was dying, but it was all right. I didn't know what he meant by paradise, but I didn't care. Somehow I knew if I was with him, it would be all right. I wanted to be with him wherever he was.

He was fading. But he seemed to summon one last surge of energy, raised up, and cried, "It is finished!"

Then he slumped back down and rested. I wasn't sure what he meant. What was finished? His life? His torture? His mission? I didn't know but I knew he was the Christ like the angel had said. He was the king. But why was he dying? I didn't know but I was glad to have seen him again and was so glad I had talked to him. He then raised his head, looked heavenward, and said, "Father, into your hands I commit my spirit," and he died.

I barely knew him and yet I cried again. I was in so much pain, in so much emotional trauma, in so much relief from talking to Jesus that I just couldn't stop crying. But as Jesus died, almost like a sign from heaven, it began to rain. The crowd was further depleted and the Romans got busy moving this ordeal along.

Then all of a sudden, the ground began to shake. Rocks were falling all around us and rolling down the barren hill and people began to stumble like they were drunk. The Roman soldiers, as well as the remaining Jews, were staggering without any control over themselves. My only thought was if the shaft I was attached to was shaken out of its place, I was going to fall straight over and be crushed from my own weight and there was nothing I could do to prevent it. But then, just as suddenly as it began, the earthquake stopped. The centurion who had noticed Jesus's passing and the rain coming down and the earthquake, made an amazing observation.

I heard him say, "Surely this man was the son of God."

That was it. Even a Roman knew it. I realized I knew it, although I hadn't declared it. Jesus was Yahweh's son. He was Yahweh who came down to earth to live with us. That's why the baby's birth was so miraculous and special! That's why the angels came to us! That's why the star was so big and bright! Mary and Joseph had Yahweh's son. And I had been given the wonderful opportunity to witness his birth, receive his blessing, and witness his death. Now my life could end. I was ready to meet Yahweh. I was ready to see Jesus again. He promised we would, and I trusted him.

As I dreamed of heaven and seeing Jesus, I was slammed back to reality by the sound of a soldier striking Daniel's legs with a huge hammer. I'm sure it broke Daniel's legs as he screamed and slumped down on the step where his feet were nailed. Next, the soldiers went to check on Jesus but realized he was dead so they didn't break his legs. Instead, one soldier thrust his spear into Jesus's side and out poured some blood and some water. He was dead. They were satisfied. Then they came to me and realized I was still conscious so they struck my legs. It hurt so bad and yet I was already in such pain that it didn't matter much more. But it did mean a great deal to my breathing. I realized very quickly what they were doing. With broken legs, I could only raise up to breathe with extreme pain. I realized I would be dead very soon. I looked over at Daniel to say good-bye and realized he was already dead. So I told Yahweh I was sorry for my life. I asked Him to watch over my mother and my wife. I thanked Him for letting me meet Jesus. Then I took my last gasp of a difficult breath and closed my eyes.

NINETEEN

I DON'T KNOW HOW LONG it was before I opened my eyes again. But when I did, the vision was completely different. In front of me was the sweetest sight I had ever seen. All I could see was Jesus. I assumed I was in paradise so I looked around. As my eyes focused, I realized how stunningly beautiful this place was. It was like a perfect garden, like paradise would be. This must be heaven. But the best part was Jesus was there. His promise was fulfilled. All the pain was gone. All the tears were gone. All the shame and humiliation was gone. There was incredible light all around me and an overwhelming feeling of love and joy encasing me as I walked toward Jesus.

As I got closer to him, his smile was radiant and his arms were outstretched to greet me. I knew it was him by his hands. The scars on his hands from the spikes were still there. There was no blood or crown of thorns but the scars told me it was him. Then I rushed to him and fell into his arms. As I wrapped my arms around his neck I saw my own scars on my hands as well. The scars of my life were not gone yet I knew I was redeemed. I would remain there forever. I was home. I was forgiven. I was with Jesus.

EPILOGUE

THROUGH NOTHING BUT THE MAGNIFICENT grace of God, I was blessed to witness God's glory in the birth of His son. I saw with my own eyes the angel, the star, and the heavenly host singing praises to the glory of Yahweh. I saw the baby Jesus in his manger. Then after a life of heartache and poor choices, I deserved only punishment and death. But, again, by the matchless grace of almighty God, I was given the privilege of sharing in the death of His son and witnessing His promise of the glory of paradise. I truly experienced "glory to glory" as only God can display it.

ABOUT THE AUTHOR

THE AUTHOR IS A PRACTICING dentist who has lived his entire life in and around Atlanta, GA. He has been married to his wife, Roxanne, for over thirty years. They have three grown boys, Andy, Christopher, and Josh. Roxanne is a church musician at a church where the author teaches Sunday School and directs the drama ministry. They reside in the mountains of north Georgia in the community of Big Canoe. They enjoy traveling and playing with their grandchild. The author also enjoys golf and walking the dog.